Joseph Sanson

Hope and Ambition

Joseph Sanson

Hope and Ambition

ISBN/EAN: 9783337090661

Printed in Europe, USA, Canada, Australia, Japan

Cover: Foto ©Andreas Hilbeck / pixelio.de

More available books at **www.hansebooks.com**

HOPE AND

DRA

IN FIVE ACTS

TO WHICH

Cast of the Characters—En
Positions of the Perfor
the whole of th

WRITTEN AND D

JOSEPH

PHIL

P

"HOPE AND AMBITION."

SYNOPSIS.

"HOPE AND AMBITION."

PROLOGUE PLAYED IN PROVIDENCE, R. I.

An Elapse of Ten Years Between First Act of Play and Prologue.

"PLAY."

A PROLOGUE AND FIVE ACTS.

Characters in Prologue.

WALTER OSGOOD, *a New England boy, aged fifteen years.*

PIERRE LIVINGSTON, *Companion of Walter, aged fourteen years.*

ANDRÉ LIVINGSTON, *Father to Pierre, and Head Clerk at Banking House of Emory, Dorman & Co.*

MRS. BLANCHARD, *Housekeeper of André Livingston.*

ARMORE DUDLEY, *Corresponding Clerk.*

CHARLES, *Clerk of Emory, Dorman & Co.*

WILLIAM, *Clerk.*

ALBERT DOUGLAS, *Clerk in one of the National Banks in Providence.*

"DRAMATIS PERSONÆ."

WALTER OSGOOD, *a New England Mechanic.*

CAPTAIN DARLINGTON, *a retired Sea Captain.*

FREDERICK DARLINGTON, *Son of Captain Darlington.*

PIERRE LIVINGSTON, *Friend of Frederick Dariington.*

GEORGE BROWNELL, *a Detective of the City of Washington.*

EDWARD SINGLETON, *assumed name of André Livingston from Prologue.*

JONATHAN SKINNER, *a Vermont Speculator.*

JIM BRAILAND, *Keeper of Gaming Saloon at Washington.*

COUNT ABREGÉ, *Officer in Russian Army.*

MARTHA OSGOOD, *Mother of Walter Osgood.*

HELEN DARLINGTON, *Daughter of Captain Darlington.*

LUCY DARLINGTON, *Wife of Captain Darlington.*

REMO, *First Officer of the Guard.*

ALDRO, *Sentinal.*

CORRUNA, *Sentinal.*

CALENDO, *Guard at Bastille.*

BOREISO, *Second Guard at Bastille.*

AGNES, *Servant Girl at Darlington's.*

Game Keeper and Gamblers at Gaming Saloon.

Waiters at Gaming Saloon.

Ladies and Gentlemen—Villagers at the House of Darlington.

Two Relief Guards at Bastille.

1*

SYNOPSIS OF SCENERY.

"PROLOGUE."

SCENE I.

Home of André Livingston.
[COMFORTABLE ROOM, NEATLY FURNISHED.]
Centre D. in F., windows each side of door looking out on the garden.

SCENE II.
Banking Office.
[THREE LARGE DESKS, IRON SAFE, LARGE CLOCK ON MANTEL PIECE]
Door in centre; door to the left; lot of books on the desks, inkstands and utensils; waste basket under each desk; hat rack.

ACT I.
SCENE.
A New England Home.
[Furniture—old style; large old-fashioned clock; large portrait of Walter's father hanging on wall.]

ACT II.
SCENE I.

Narrow Street in the City of Washington.

SCENE II.

A Beautiful Large Parlor.

[Chandelier in middle of room; side lights; large mirrors; waiters running to and fro, dressed in scarlet uniforms; large table in back-ground, with gambling implements; two small tables on the side occupied by different card-players.

At large table four gentlemen engaged in playing faro—two of whom are Frederick Darlington and Pierre Livingston.]

ACT III.

SCENE.

Home of Captain Darlington.

[Parlor, elegantly furnished; door in centre; two windows each side of door; clock on mantel piece.]

ACT IV.

SCENE I.

Snowing.—Palace Square at St. Petersburgh; in background a large Wall, representing Palace Wall.

[Two sentinels walking in front of the wall of the Palace, meeting each other at intervals; two large lamps in front of Palace; door in centre of wall.]

SCENE II.

Narrow Stage, representing Front of a Prison.

[Two doors in flat, right and left, the left door to have a wicket in it.]

ACT V.

SCENE.

Home of Captain Darlington.

[Same as Scene in Act III.]

[In addition to Scene in Act III, a table with refreshments and bouquet of flowers; door in centre; two windows each side of door.]

PROLOGUE.

SCENE I.—HOME OF ANDRÉ LIVINGSTON. [*Comfortable room, neatly furnished, (D. C. flat,). Window to the right, looking towards garden, D. on right; also, window to the left.*]

ANDRÉ. One month this day, I buried my wife. How desolate my home is now—how strange everything seems to me—those pleasant days I have spent with her here are no more. Oh! dear Alice, how sad I feel. All I have now left to comfort me is my son Pierre. What will become of you now? To-day I stand here a criminal; brought on by financial embarrassment. Why have I misused the confidence of my employers? I have been for ten years the head clerk of the house of Emory, Dorman & Co., and I have committed a forgery. Shame and disgrace will follow me; and as to my son, the world will look on him with scorn. I must fly from here before I am detected, and seek refuge in some foreign land. I will work, toil, to atone for my crime, and some day I may be able to convince the world that André Livingston has tried to regain the confidence of his former friends.

I cannot delay, as before the closing of the bank to-morrow all will be detected.—Some one is coming.

[PIERRE *enters from C. D. in Flat, from the garden.*]

PIERRE. Dear father I have been looking for you in the garden; I am so happy to see you; I feel so lonely since my dear mother died; her sweet voice, her kind carresses, all are gone from me now. O, dear mother, I wish I was with you in Heaven. Father, Walter Osgood has been with me part of the morning in the garden.

ANDRÉ. Well, my son, he is a good boy and a noble companion for you.

PIERRE. He is always talking about machinery, and building castles in the air about something of a secret to find some new invention, and I being brought up in a collegiate education, what do I know about such things?

ANDRÉ. This is great credit for Walter. It is no shame or disgrace to be a mechanic, it is an honor. What would the world be as to progress if not for mechanics. Where are those happy days when I was a mechanic,—those days are past and never to return.

PIERRE. (*Looking out the window towards the garden.*) Here comes our good old housekeeper, Mrs. Blanchard.

[MRS. BLANCHARD *enters from C. D. F.*]

MRS. BLANCHARD. Good morning, Mr. Livingston; you will please tell Pierre not to be so wild when he is in company with Walter; he is such a good boy, but Pierre is so rude.

PIERRE. Why, Mrs. Blanchard, you are always complaining to father about my conduct; remember you have been young yourself.

ANDRÉ. You must obey and respect Mrs. Blanchard. Your dear mother is dead. Take her counsel, be obedient, and accept her kind advice, and no doubt some future day you will be thankful to her and then appreciate how valuable her lessons were to you.

PIERRE. Father, dear, I will obey Mrs. Blanchard in the future. How long Walter stays, he promised me to ask of you a favor, and no doubt you will grant his request.

MRS. BLANCHARD. (*Looking out of the window.*) Here comes our little friend Walter.

[WALTER *enters from C. D. F.*]

WALTER. Good morning, Mr. Livingston, Mrs. Blanchard; are you both well? I came here, sir, to ask you if you will permit Pierre to spend the afternoon with me. I made some new drawings, and would like him to examine them.

ANDRÉ. It is always a great pleasure to me for Pierre to be with you. I know you are a good companion for him.

WALTER. Sir, I am obliged to you.

PIERRE. I thank you father, you will allow me then to go with Walter—you are so kind. (*Takes his hat from the chair, joining WALTER in the act of leaving.*)

ANDRÉ. Pierre, take a father's blessing. (*Kissing him.*) (*Aside.*) This may be the last I will ever see you again.

PIERRE. You tremble father,—how strange you look. Oh what a feeling comes over me just now.

ANDRÉ. Pierre, my dear boy, I am well, but the recollection of the past, and my future prospects, make me feel nervous.

WALTER. Let us go now, mother has expected me long before this.

PIERRE. I will go with you, but I hate to leave father, he seems
so strange.

ANDRÉ. Pierre, my son, some business of importance calls me
away from home for a few days. Mrs. Blanchard will stay with you,
and when I return, and your conduct has been without reproach, I will
bring you and Walter some presents. Come to my arms and receive a
father's blessing.

PIERRE. Don't stay long, dear father, we will be so lonely without
you. (*Reaching his hand to* WALTER.) Come, let us go. (*Kissing
his father.* WALTER *and* PIERRE *exit, by door Right.*)

ANDRE. (*Looking after them.*) May God guide you, and have a
father's blessing. (*Turning towards* MRS. BLANCHARD *and taking a
large wallet from his pocket.*) Mrs. Blanchard, you have been with us
for many years. My dear wife respected you as a friend and a companion—as to me, I always look to you as a mother, and I have to
leave Pierre in your care for some time, as important business calls me
to go abroad. You will find in this book sufficient money for some
time for you and Pierre, and for his future education.

MRS. BLANCHARD. You know well the responsibility that would
rest with me to have the care of Pierre; one that requires constantly the watchful eye of a father.

ANDRÉ. I cannot stay with you; I must leave; my honor and
reputation are at stake, and the future welfare of my only boy is de-
pending on it.

MRS. BLANCHARD. This is some joke of yours—you will tell me
what all this means.

ANDRÉ. No one knows of this, but oh, God! to-morrow all will be
lost. (*Blushing, holding his hands on his face and turning away from*
MRS. BLANCHARD.) Shame! disgrace! dishonor!—I have committed
a forgery.

MRS. BLANCHARD. Oh! my God! has it come to this? The once
noble and worthy André Livingston to stand here a self-confessed
criminal.

ANDRÉ. Mrs. Blanchard, for the respect and honor you have always had for my dear departed wife and towards me, do not condemn
me thus, and listen :—Persuaded by bad counsel I bought stocks and
used the money of my employers, with bright hopes, but, alas, those
hopes became cloudy and then—you know all.

MRS. BLANCHARD. You have so many influential friends here, cannot they assist you ? and remain at home with us. Go see them and
tell them all.

ANDRÉ. No, the shame and remorse! I cannot approach them.
What a coward is a man after he has committed a false step? But I

trust my son Pierre will not be disgraced by the acts of his father.

MRS. BLANCHARD. Go, André Livingston, leave your once honorable and happy home before it is too late. I understand all. Don't let dishonor dwell here beneath that roof from which your dear wife departed her pure soul, and don't let your child know the errors of his father.

ANDRÉ. Mrs. Blanchard, be a mother to Pierre, and may the blessings of Heaven be on you and my child. I will work and toil, and hope one day to return and be worthy of this once happy home again. I will then receive my Pierre in my open arms and be worthy again to be called father. (*Throwing his arms around* MRS. BLANCHARD'S *neck, kisses her over and over again.*) Farewell! May God be with you and Pierre.

[*Exit by R. D.,* MRS. BLANCHARD *looking after him in tears.*]

END OF FIRST SCENE OF PROLOGUE.

SCENE II.—BANKING OFFICE.—[*Three large desks, iron safe, large clock on mantel-piece. D. in F. Door to the left. Window in F. to right, looking out to road. Large lot of books on different desks, pens, inkstands, waste-baskets under desks. Hat-rack.*]

ARMORE. Charles, it is now two o'clock, and André has not made his appearance, and there is some correspondence to be finished to-day.

CHARLES. I do pity him; there is a great change in him of late, since he lost his wife, he is so melancholy.

WILLIAM. I have observed the same in André's conduct. Let us place ourselves in his position, and would we not be the same. When he left here yesterday he acted so strangely.

ARMORE. I expect Mr. Emory here soon, he said he would be here before the bank closes. It is steamer day to-morrow, and we have to send large remittances abroad.

CHARLES. I will look out and see if he is coming. (*Going towards the window looking towards the road.*) He is coming.

[MR. EMORY *enters from door in Flat.*]

MR. EMORY. Good morning, gentlemen. Why, where is André Livingston?

ARMORE. He has not been here this morning.

EMORY. Send a messenger forthwith to his house, and learn the cause of his absence.

ARMORE. William, will you please go.

WILLIAM. I will, sir. (*Exit by D. in F.*)

EMORY. Armore, what amount have we to send drafts for?

ARMORE. A large amount, sir.

EMORY. More than usual?

ARMORE. Yes sir. By the last steamer our remittances were of a great deal less amount than they are to-day.

[WILLIAM *enters D. in F.*]

EMORY. Have you any news.

WILLIAM. (*Looking pale.*) I have, but I am afraid it is bad news. André Livingston has fled the country.

EMORY. What means this. How are his accounts?

ARMORE. This will take some time to look after.

[*Enter* ALBERT DOUGLAS, *D. in F.*]

ALBERT. You are Mr. Emory, I believe, sir?

EMORY. Yes sir, and what do you want. (*Excited.*)

ALBERT. A forgery to a large extent has just been discovered in our bank, and came from your house, and made by some of your clerks.

EMORY. I see it all—misplaced confidence—and by no one else than by André Livingston. And what is the amount?

ALBERT. Here, sir, are the documents. (*Handing* MR. EMORY *some papers.*)

EMORY. O, Heavens, is it possible—thirty thousand dollars! Where is the villain? Report immediately to the office of the detective bureau. Let all steamers and railroad stations be watched. Give his description and offer five thousand dollars reward for his arrest.

ARMORE. I will attend to it forthwith. (*Exit by D. in F.*)

EMORY. My partners have always told me that I trusted far more confidence in my clerks than I should have done. (*Exit by door Left.*)

WILLIAM. May the criminal be brought to justice.

[*Curtain Drops.*]

END OF PROLOGUE.

ACT I.

SCENE I.—A NEW ENGLAND HOME; *furniture old style, large old-fashioned clock. Large Portrait of Walter's father on wall of back flat. (Door in C. D. F.) Two old-fashioned sofas on each side of Stage. Large arm chair. Spin-wheel.*

WALTER. One year to-day my father died, and having tried all possible means, but it seems luck runs against me, and it seems of no use,—I must leave for some foreign port, and hope there to succeed, and then I will be able to keep that sacred promise I gave my father in his last hour,—that I should take his part and look to the comfort of my dear mother.

[MRS. OSGOOD *enters from 3 L. E.*]

MRS. OSGOOD. Dear Walter, how strange you look this morning, what is the cause? Of late you seem so melancholy. You are always thinking of some new plan. My dear son, it is of no use building castles in the air.

WALTER. Mother, I am young and will not spend my useful days here any longer. I will seek for future prospects in some foreign land, and will work from early morn 'till late at night for your comfort, and to care for you as I have promised my dear departed father. I cannot perform that solemn obligation, as prospects here are so gloomy to me, and I hope to receive your kind blessing when I will return, and then my hopes may be realized to make Helen Darlington my own dear wife.

MRS. OSGOOD. I do believe, most sincerely, that of late you have neglected everything, and your mind is altogether on Helen, and this may be the cause of your reverse in business.

WALTER. I do confess to you I think of her I so dearly love and adore, but what can I expect of the future under present circumstances. You accused me wrongly, I never neglected my business, but future hopes are at present my only thoughts.

MRS. OSGOOD. Do not look at present for any more than our humble circumstances will permit. My son, riches do not make a home happy, but contentment. Trust in our Creator and then your future path, I hope, will be bright.

WALTER. Nothing can change my mind; I am resolute, nay daring, and this very day I will leave this home of my boyhood, and you, dear mother, all I have now on this earth I so dearly love and honor;— and as to Helen, time will tell.

2

MRS. OSGOOD.   Some one is coming.

[*Enter* HELEN *3 R. E.*]

HELEN.   Good morning, Mrs. Osgood; Good morning Walter; we have a beautiful day—but how strange you look!

MRS. OSGOOD.   Helen, my dear, Walter has changed so much of late, he is always so downcast; he has not that ambition he formerly had, and is always making some new plans. There is some secret in his heart and you may be able to get him to reveal it to you.

WALTER.   Mother, do not burden Helen's heart with my misfortunes; she is so good and pure, spare her that pain.

HELEN.   Why, Walter, I always spoke of you among my friends, as I believed that you are, one of the happiest and most contented young men in our city.

WALTER.   I was once, but those happy days are past.

HELEN.   And why? It is not me, I hope, that caused you all these unhappy thoughts? You seem nervous.

WALTER.   How could you cause this? Your very presence always brightens my hopes for our future, but don't let us talk any more on this subject. Have you heard of late of your brother Frederick, who left home without the least cause?

HELEN.   No, Walter, we have not, but you knew Fred. from boyhood had always a roving disposition, and he always spoke of leaving home. He was always independent of the world; the mind of a true young American. If he only does not find vile associates, and lead a reckless life, we will hope for the best, and that on some future day all may come right.

MRS. OSGOOD.   Helen, I have for some time past promised your good mother a visit, let us go and we will leave Walter; I will not be long, and shall return soon.

WALTER.   Mother, go with Helen. Keep your promise to return soon.

[*Exeunt* HELEN *and* MRS. OSGOOD *by 3 L. E.*]

WALTER.   If this girl would only know how sincerely I love her; she is an angel; I only wish that my future days may be bright and my hopes realized to call her my own dear wife. I will be no coward. This day I will take my departure from home, and return a man worthy of the hand of Helen Darlington.

My father has often told me that if we could only discover the secret of making the Russian iron in this country our fortune would be made, but it is only known there, and there made by convicts condemned for life servitude—how to get at this. But there is no such

word as fail. We young Americans are cunning, and for that country
I will start. No doubt there may be some danger in all this, but what
of that? To conquer my object I will not fail. My heart beats and
tells me—Walter, you will be the conqueror. I am resolved, and
nothing will keep me back. Let me look on my father's picture. His
expression even now on that canvas is so mild and intelligent. Oh!
dear father! could you but listen to my words and give me your counsel I have always so dearly appreciated. O, God! may your pure soul
be in that celestial home, and that the angels of Peace be gathered
'round you and listen to my prayers. May I be protected from all
dangers on the long journey I have before me, and the blessing of
Heaven be on my dear mother and Helen, and spare them from all
evil until my return. Amen!

[*Enter* Mrs. Osgood *from 3 L. E.*]

Mrs. Osgood. Walter, my visit to the Darlington family has been
very pleasant indeed. Mrs. Darlington is such a kind lady, and the
old captain, why he is so pleasant. They have expressed themselves
in a way no doubt they will give their consent to your marriage with
Helen. They seem so happy.

Walter. You did not tell them of my plan?

Mrs. Osgood. Why, no, how silly you are, to be sure. You have
tears in your eyes.

Walter. Mother, during your absence I have been looking at
my father's portrait, and how could a son with the expectation of
leaving his once happy home do this without shedding tears.

Mrs. Osgood. You are then determined to leave home. It may
be humble, but better to remain here than to be away from that virtu-
ous roof where your dear father has always tried to teach you one
day to become an upright man, and a good, devoted Christian. You
are my only joy now left in this world, and will you leave your poor
old mother?

Walter. Mother, you know from boyhood my ambition was always to rise in the world, and not to remain what I am now. My
future here looks gloomy, and a few years separation from you, and
from her I so dearly love, may bring me back to your arms, so that I
may be able to be a pride to both of you. Ocean and land may separate us, but a son's love towards his mother cannot. Mother, many
younger men than I have left their homes with bright hopes, and were
successful, and why should I fail to bring back honor and fortune to
you both, and then I will be the happiest man in this world.

Mrs. Osgood. (*Coming near Walter, taking her two hands and
giving him her blessing—looking up to Heaven.*) May God be your

guide, and accept the blessing of a devoted mother; but Walter, remain
with me, as old as I am, I would rather work and toil for thee from
early morn 'till late at night, than you to be separated from me. You
will get the consent of Helen's parents and she is such a noble girl—I
know she would rather share with you even that humble home, than
for you to leave us, it may be never to behold you again. But let me
beg of you to stay with us and then we will all be so happy.

WALTER. Happy did you say, how could I be, until that time will
come when I can give you and Helen all comforts due to you, and
then I hope to deserve your esteem, and Helen's love. Mother I am
determined and resolved, and nothing will keep me back.

MRS. OSGOOD. Walter, then you are resolute and may you have
that success you so richly deserve.

WALTER. The time will soon pass, and I will return and then hope
to be a pride to you. As to my duty, when I will be abroad, I will
never forget as long as I live.

MRS. OSGOOD. Captain Darlington says he will be here to-day, and
we may look for him soon.

[WALTER *looking out of the window.*]

WALTER. I hear the carriage approaching, they are coming.

[CAPT. DARLINGTON, LUCY DARLINGTON *and* HELEN *enter C. D.
in F.*]

WALTER. Captain, Mrs. Darlington, Helen, you are welcome.

CAPT. DARLINGTON. Walter, I promised your mother to pay you a
visit. She told me you were not the same young man you were formerly. What is the cause, tell me. I am your friend, and possibly may
aid you.

WALTER. I thank you. Mother thinks me wrong, only my hopes
look towards the future, and as to ambition I have within my very
soul, all will come out right.

MRS. DARLINGTON. (*Aside to Captain.*) Every line on this young
man's forehead denotes he is in love.

CAPTAIN. Always your old ways, to know other people's business.

MRS. DARLINGTON. (*Approaching her husband.*) My dear Captain, well do I recollect my mother used to say to me, "why Lucy, you
are not the same girl you were formerly, since you are in love,"—but
those days are past, ain't they Captain.

CAPTAIN. I should think about time, don't you, darling?

MRS. DARLINGTON. Why, we are'nt so old yet.

CAPTAIN. Well, I don't know; both of us count a pretty nice round sum,—one hundred and ten. Our spring chicken days are pretty well over.

HELEN. Father, I feel so strange to day, as if something was going to happen.

CAPTAIN. Dear girl, don't be so foolish. No use talking, she is the same as Lucy was when she had her age.

HELEN. Father, you speak to Walter, do for my sake, and you may persuade him to remain with us. He is young, and a good mechanic, and his prospects are as good here as in a foreign land.

MRS. OSGOOD. Dear Helen, Walter has resolved to leave home this day.

HELEN. (*Approaching towards her father.*) Father, do me the favor I asked of you a few minutes ago.

CAPTAIN. Dear Helen, I will do all in my power for you, also for Walter, but I encourage a young man that has ambition to rise in the world.

MRS. OSGOOD. Captain Darlington, oh, sir, how unfortunate I am to part with my only child and protector, one I so dearly love. You have a son, although you have not heard from him for years, but place yourself in my present circumstances, would you not have these same feelings. Speak to him as if he were your own son, and I implore you try to convince him of his youthful and thoughtless plans.

HELEN. Father, Walter's noble mind is always on a higher station in life, but I am contented in his present lot. I will work and toil with him, whatever his destiny may be in future I will most happily share with him; nay, even in poverty, if he only remains with us.

CAPTAIN. Helen, you are a most noble girl, and deserving of one who will make you happy. We have great respect for Walter, and he is worthy of the love you have for him, and no doubt the happy day for both of you will not be long distant. I glory in his spirit, and he will not make you his wife until he can give you such comfort in married life you so richly deserve in every respect.

HELEN. Oh! father, the time will be so long if Walter leaves, but let us hope of his speedy return, and we all will be happy.

WALTER. (*To* CAPTAIN.) As you have honored me with your visit this morning, I have to inform you that I have resolved to leave home this day, and to part with those I so dearly love; but my manly duty demands this sacrifice. When I return and be worthy of your esteem may I then ask your consent to make your daughter my wife?

CAPTAIN. Walter you have mine and her mother's consent, and when the time shall arrive, may you both be happy.

WALTER. (*Rushing towards his mother.*) Now mother, your consent I have I know well, and dear Helen, as to you, this day I will

2*

never forget, and when I return I hope to be worthy of your kind love and affection.

HELEN.   Walter, my happiness would be complete if you could only stay with us, but as you are determined, I will look forward to your return as the happiest day in my life, and will never forget the sacrifice you make for me in leaving your good old mother.

WALTER.   I am going to leave, and with the hopes I have for my future, the time will soon pass 'till I receive you all again in my open arms, and receive your blessings.

CAPTAIN.   Walter, I like a young man of your stripe.

WALTER.   Seeking fortunes is all very well, but those I leave behind me,—God only knows if I ever will behold any of them I so dearly love.

CAPTAIN   Pshaw, pshaw,—no such doubts.   We old sea captains don't think of those foolish thoughts.

MRS. OSGOOD.   Walter, my boy, come to my arms; this day I will always remember while I live.   It is a sorrowful day for me to part with you I so dearly love.

[*Parting Scene.* WALTER *in tears,* MRS. OSGOOD *and* HELEN *close to* WALTER.]

WALTER.   Dear mother, the most critical moment of my life has almost arrived.   I have to leave you, but my resolutions are as firm as a rock.   Let me say farewell to you all, and, O God, listen to my prayer—Watch over my dear mother, let no danger befall her, and let the guardian angel be with her.   Helen, love, may the bright star of Heaven always shine on thee; and remember him who so dearly loves you.   My thoughts by day, and my dreams by night, will be for you, and, remember, my promise I will solemnly keep.

[WALTER *embraces his mother and* HELEN, *and receives the blessing of his mother.*]

CAPTAIN.   Walter, as I have some business in Washington, I will go with you as far as New York, and see you off when the steamer sails.

WALTER.   Your kindness to me will always be appreciated.   Now, mother, Helen, Mrs. Darlington, farewell.   (*Rushing from them,* CAPTAIN DARLINGTON *following* WALTER.)   God bless you all.

[WALTER *and* CAPTAIN *exit by* C. D. F.   HELEN *and* MRS. OSGOOD
       both fall.   Curtain drops.]

END OF ACT I.

ACT II.

THE SURPRISE.

SCENE I.—NARROW STREET IN CITY OF WASHINGTON.   (*D. in F.*)
Enter CAPTAIN DARLINGTON, *1 L. E.*

CAPTAIN.   There is certainly a great change in this city.   It is about five and twenty years since I was here last.

I must say for an old seaman I did feel worked up when I left New York yesterday after seeing my friend Walter off.   May he arrive safely at his destination.

[*Enter* GEORGE BROWNELL, *1 R. E., and in hurry passes* CAPTAIN.]

CAPTAIN.   Fine morning, sir!

GEORGE.   Most delightful.

CAPTAIN.   Would you inform me of a good hotel to stop at.   I have not been here for many years, and have lost run of them.

GEORGE.   (*Aside, detective-like, inquisitive about everyone's business.*) Are you going to make a long stay?

CAPTAIN.   Silent tongues, sir, makes wise heads.

GEORGE   (*Aside.*)   This fellow is no fool.

CAPTAIN.   Did I understand you to say I am a fool.

GEORGE.   No, sir; I beg pardon; I said what a fool a man is to meddle with other people's affairs.

CAPTAIN.   Now, my boy, you talk sense.

GEORGE.   (*Taking out his watch.*)   I must leave—almost twelve o'clock.

CAPTAIN.   Well, sir, the name of the hotel.

GEORGE.   Globe Hotel.

CAPTAIN.   Be kind enough and give me some information in regard to some government business of mine in this city.

JONATHAN.   [*Enters from 1 L. E.   Knife and stick in hand whittling.*]   Good day gentlemen, I am from down east, and have been in Washington three days, and don't know as much now as I did when I came, by Jove.

CAPTAIN.   What part of the east did you come from ?

JONATHAN.   From the greatest State in the Union—Vermont.

GEORGE.   And what brings you here ?

JONATHAN.   My grandfather had some land given to him by the government many years ago, and I came here to Washington to find if the land is somewhere in the far West, but no one seems to know anything about my grandfather, Jeremiah Skinner, Esq., and I have made up my mind that they are all pudding heads here. We call them at home state puddlers.

CAPTAIN.   Your education, I see, has not been neglected, to use such high grammar as pudding heads and state puddlers.

JONATHAN.   By Jove, talk about education, the first thing we learn in our great schools in Vermont, is A B C, and after we know them we are considered quite a scholar, and I am glad you notice and appreciate a man of my abilities, by Jove.

GEORGE.   Captain, you will excuse me for about half an hour, I have some important business to attend.

CAPTAIN.   I will wait your return here.

JONATHAN.   So will I, by Jove.

[GEORGE *exit by 1 L. E.*]

JONATHAN.   This seems to be a smart duck.   What do you think of him ?

CAPTAIN.   You had better look out here in this great city, they are pretty sharp.

JONATHAN.   I say old Commodore, or Captain, I came here also to see the sights ; you know what I mean, and I have a considerable amount of greenbacks with me, and I'm not going to be sharp't out of them. Look here, old fellow, you seem to have a straight, upright countenance, suppose you save my money until I go home.

CAPTAIN.   I am a stranger to you, and who knows but what I might spend your cash.

JONATHAN.   By Jove, if you do you are a dead Commodore. (*Takes a large wallet from his pocket, handing it to the Captain.*) Here, my friend, keep this wallet, take good care of it, as it contains the large amount of eleven dollars. That ought to be enough to see a man through.

CAPTAIN.   This is certainly a large amount.

JONATHAN.   I say, captain, as I promised to take our chambermaid to a ball to-night, let me have a dollar out of my cash.

CAPTAIN.   Let me count your money. [*Captain looking over the notes.*] This two dollar bill is a counterfeit.

JONATHAN.   The miserable creature ! Why, I got this from the

pie-woman in the market; I'll go right back; give me the note. By
Jove, I'll have satisfaction, or my name ain't Jonathan Skinner.

[JONATHAN, *exit 1 L. E.*]

CAPTAIN.   My friend George's half hour is nearly up.   Ah, here
he comes.

[GEORGE *enters from 1 L. E.*]

CAPTAIN.   You kept your word.

GEORGE.   May I ask you your name?

CAPTAIN.   My name, sir? Captain Darlington, of Providence, Rhode
Island.   And what business are *you* engaged in?

GEORGE.   I am a detective in this city.

CAPTAIN.   Old boy—beg pardon, but this is my way of speaking,
as an old seaman—Mr. Detective, you may be of some service to me.

GEORGE.   (*Aside.*)   Thousands in it.

CAPTAIN.   What did you say?

GEORGE.   Be pleased to be of any service to you.   (*Looking
around.*)   We are alone, sir; please proceed.

CAPTAIN.   My friend, you are a married man, no doubt?

GEORGE.   Do I look like a married man?   Yes, I have been, but I
left my sweet angel of a wife.

CAPTAIN.   And on what account?

GEORGE.   The old story—my mother-in-law wanted to be chief cook
and bottle washer, and Georgie could not see it in that light.

CAPTAIN.   Have you any children?

GEORGE.   No, sir! and a most fortunate circumstance.

CAPTAIN.   Well now to business.   My visit in Washington is in re-
lation to some government affairs, as I told you before, but while I am
here, could you not find a young man, among your so-called " fast
men," named Frederick Darlington?

GEORGE.   By Jove, that is the boy—the name in my diary.   (*Aside.*)
Now for biz.

CAPTAIN.   What boy?

GEORGE.   We detectives don't care for our services—to be paid for
what we do, O no! but still a little present we don't mind, no compul-
sion, sir.

CAPTAIN.   I will reward you five hundred dollars if you can restore
to me my long lost son.

[JONATHAN *enters from 1 L. E.   Comes rushing in with a two dollar
note in his hand.*]

JONATHAN.   Here I am, no use to look for me.

CAPTAIN. Jonathan I have some business with this gentleman, keep silent.

JONATHAN. I was going to ring the pie woman's nose off if she hadn't forked out solid spondulix, by Jove.

CAPTAIN. I'm pleased she did.

[JONATHAN *sits down on the floor, whittles a stick.*]

GEORGE. And the name of your son.

CAPTAIN. Frederick Darlington.

GEORGE. Frederick Darlington your son?

CAPTAIN. Yes sir, and why so astonished?

GEORGE—Because—O don't know.

CAPTAIN. For the worst, tell me all.

GEORGE. Your son, Frederick Darlington, is a noted gambler.

CAPTAIN. Can this be possible—the care I bestowed upon him when a boy—my son a gambler—how can I inform his mother who so dearly loves him, of this dreadful news?

GEORGE. Do as I did. I never told my wife anything, except I wanted to tell her.

CAPTAIN. No sir! what I know, my wife must know.

GEORGE. (*Aside.*) One of those old silly fools.

CAPTAIN. Now sir, the proof of all this.

GEORGE—So said, so done. Meet me to-night at 8, precisely, at "E" street, and we will go to "Brailand's Gaming House," and there we may find him engaged in his hellish work.

CAPTAIN. I will be there.

GEORGE. Recollect, 8, at "E."

[GEORGE *exit 1 R. E.*]

JONATHAN. Here Captain, take this two dollar note with the other bulk of my money, and by Jove I'll be there to-night. I overheard all you said, Captain, you and that other duck, be sure and meet at 8, A, B, C, D, E, street; I'll be there, or my name ain't Jonathan Skinner.

[CAPTAIN *exit,* JONATHAN *following.*]

SCENE II.—BEAUTIFUL LARGE PARLOR; *chandelier in middle of room, side lights, large mirrors; waiters running to and fro dressed in scarlet uniforms; large table in back ground with gaming implements; two small tables on the side occupied by different card-players; at large table dealer and four gentlemen engaged in playing faro, two of them* FREDERICK DARLINGTON *and* PIERRE LIVINGSTON.

[*D. in F. Enter* GEORGE BROWNELL; *and* CAPTAIN DARLINGTON *disguised with long gray beard and wig on, from C. D. in F.*]

WAITER. Take your hats, gentlemen?

CAPTAIN. Never mind. (*Walks towards the large table.*)

GEORGE. (*Walking around and looking at the pictures.*) (*Aside.*) I see him, but I will work this game on a new plan. (*Walks towards* CAPTAIN.) You go there and buy some of those white bones (*Giving the dealer some money,*) and commence to play and be on the watch. (*Aside.*) This new game of mine will work 500 slugs.

[JONATHAN *enters from C. D. Flat.*]

JONATHAN. By Jove, what a place, (*Looking around.*) This is the place our folks talk about, this must be Congress or the White House. O! look at the large candle-sticks! (*Pointing to the chandeliers.*)

WAITER. (*Going towards* JONATHAN.) Your hat, sir.

JONATHAN. No sir-ree, by Jove this hat is good enough for years to come. See here blackey, what are those fellows doing here?

WAITER. Playing cards, sir.

JONATHAN. I say fellers, I can beat any man in this crowd, seven-up, for 10c. a game.

GEORGE. (*Aside.*) Here is that cursed fool, he may spoil all.

JONATHAN. (*Looking around and seeing* CAPTAIN *goes towards him.*) I know him by his looks, ah! he's dressed differently. Something up. I say old Captain, give me another dollar, I may want to speculate.

CAPTAIN. Silence sir, I'll talk to you by-and-by.

JONATHAN. Before you go and invest your cash, what is your name?

CAPTAIN. (*Aside.*) Never mind now.

JONATHAN. See here Mister, I want my money back.

CAPTAIN. (*Taking* JONATHAN *aside.*) I come here to find some one.

JONATHAN.   O by Jove, he comes here to find my land, go on old Commodore !

CAPTAIN.   (*Walks over to the gaming table and takes a note from his pocket.*)   Please hand me some of those bones.

JONATHAN.   (*Going towards the table.*)   If they don't play for dead folk's bones you can shoot me, none of that for me.   I play for the hard cash.

[*Dealer hands chips to* CAPTAIN.]

FREDERICK.   Pierre, this new comer is a green hand—a country-man.   Let us watch him, there may be something in it.

CAPTAIN.   (*Aside.*)   I cannot recognize my boy here, but the absence of many years makes a great difference.   This may be only a mistake of George's.

[*Puts part of his chips on a card.*]

DEALER.   King loses, nine wins.

CAPTAIN.   Lost, try again.   I play the seven.

DEALER.   Queen wins, the seven loses.

CAPTAIN.   I will try fifty dollars more.

DEALER.   Better luck next time.

FREDERICK.   Pierre, this old boy seems to have the stamps.

CAPTAIN.   All on the ten.

DEALER.   Ten loses, the four wins.

CAPTAIN.   My God, my last is gone now; what shall I do?   Loan me fifty dollars on my watch.

JONATHAN.   Why, Captain, you ain't up in a balloon.   Look here, take my money, and if that is gone (*Taking a large silver watch from his pocket,*) you can use this.

CAPTAIN.   Never mind, my boy; you are poor and away from home.

JONATHAN.   See here, Captain, I'm not poor, I have a farm in Vermont, twelve pigs, sixteen cows, lame horse, and two goats.   I ain't poor.

CAPTAIN.   (*To dealer of game.*)   Will you loan me fifty dollars on my watch?

DEALER.   We never loan money here on anything of the kind.

FREDERICK.   Old man, let me look at your "super."

CAPTAIN.   What do you mean by "super?"

FREDERICK.   A by-word we have among the boys for watch.

CAPTAIN.   Well, here, look at it.   (*Takes his watch from his pocket.*)

FREDERICK.   (*Looking at watch, jumps from his seat and runs to-*

wards the CAPTAIN *and takes hold of him.*) Where did you get this watch? The name of my father is on it, and it belongs to him.

CAPTAIN. (*Taking off his wig and whiskers.*) It is your father—come to my arms, my long lost son.

[*All rise from the tables.*]

GEORGE. (*Coming near the father and son.*) Never mind the five hundred dollars, this picture is reward enough for me.

FREDERICK. (*Still embracing his father.*) Father, the angels of Heaven have sent you to me, and to save me from this most horrid life. Let us leave here and take me to my home, to my dear mother, and I will explain all my long silence.

JONATHAN. By Jove, Captain, take us all home to our mothers. I want to go home and see my Ma.

CAPTAIN. O, Frederick! this is one of the happiest days in my life—to bring you to your dear mother and sister.

FREDERICK. Father, ône favor I have to ask you. Allow me to introduce to you my friend Pierre Livingston, a young man from our city; his father you have known for years. Take him with us that he may be spared this most unfortunate life.

CAPTAIN. God has sent me here to save you from destruction, why should I not save this ¯young man from the same. I will be most happy to do so.

Now gentlemen, these two young men will no longer be slaves to the gaming table, but their future will be *honesty* and *industry.*

GEORGE. Bravo! bravo! Captain, don't forget, before you leave, the $500.

CAPTAIN. No sir, you have deserved it most nobly. (CAPTAIN *handing* GEORGE *some bank notes.*)

GEORGE. I am yours most obedient.

JONATHAN. So he has deserved it. By Jove, goose me if I know what he means, that old Captain; but see here Commodore, you will not leave me behind; have you any daughters at home, I am the match for some of them. I followed you as far as the Cape of Good Fortune. O! by Jove, I mean Cape of Good Hope.

[CAPTAIN, FREDERICK, PIERRE, JONATHAN, GEORGE, *exit by C. D. F.*]

[END OF ACT II.]

3

ACT III.

THE ARRIVAL.

[HOME OF CAPTAIN DARLINGTON.—*Parlor elegantly furnished. Door in middle of flat, two windows each side of door looking out on the road. Clock on mantel-piece, bell on the table.* HELEN *sitting near table, sewing.*]

HELEN.   I wish mother would come back soon from the post-office. I am so anxious to receive a letter from Walter; it is hardly time, but waiting always makes it seem so long.

[*Enter* MRS. DARLINGTON *by C. D. in F.*]

MRS. DARLINGTON.   Dear Helen, I have brought you a letter.
HELEN.   A letter, mother!   (*In great joy running towards her.*) O do give it me.   From whom?
MRS. DARLINGTON.   From your dear father.   (HELEN *greatly disappointed turns away from her mother.*)
MRS. DARLINGTON.   Why Helen—you so disappointed, you should be glad to hear news from your father.
HELEN.   You know I am glad to hear from father, but mother, you were in love once were you not, and ——
MRS. DARLINGTON.   And what?
HELEN.   I thought the letter might have been from Walter.
MRS. DARLINGTON.   You are a foolish girl.   When will you get good sense, always thinking and talking about Walter.   There are plenty worthy young men here who would make you a good husband.
HELEN.   Mother, don't speak to me thus.   Walter is my first and only love, and one like him I can never find.   Who could take the place in my heart he does.   He is noble.   Nay! he is all the world to me, and nothing can separate us from each other in this world, but death, and death alone.

[MRS. DARLINGTON *takes a chair and sits down.*]

MRS. DARLINGTON.   Helen dear, sit by my side.

[HELEN *takes a chair and sits next to her mother.*]

HELEN. Mother give me the letter. I will read it for you.

MRS. DARLINGTON. (*Taking the letter from her pocket.*) Here it is.

[HELEN *opens the letter and looking over it, with great joy repeats the word " brother," three or four times.*]

MRS. DARLINGTON. Why don't you go on and read it for me.

HELEN. Oh dear mother, I am so joyful.

[*Reads the letter aloud.*]

" *Dear wife and daughter* :—I hope you both enjoy perfect health.
" I am well and doing well. My stay here is of a longer duration than
" I expected when I left home, but it has not been my government af-
" fairs that kept me, but a great deal more interesting matter to us
" all. I have found our long lost son, Frederick, and mother, what a
" boy he is—since he left his face looks like a dumpling, his cheeks
" rosy, his nose like yours, his actions like his father's, always to take
" good advice. I am overcome with joy. I cannot write any more.
" We will be home to-morrow. What a blessing for you, dear Lucy, to
" receive your only son once more, after such a long absence; and for
" our Helen, her brother whom she so dearly loved. A friend of
" Frederick's will come with us. No more at present,
                    Your loving husband and father,
                                        DARLINGTON.

MRS. DARLINGTON. Oh Helen!—what a joyful day for us to receive such good news. I wish it were to-morrow already.

[*Both rise and put chairs aside.*]

HELEN. Mother let us get up real early and fix everything nice,
and let us have a holiday.

MRS. DARLINGTON. All our neighbors shall be here, and we will
have quite a feast. Now that I know they are coming, every hour
seems a day to me.

[HELEN *going towards the window back part of stage.*]

HELEN. O mother ! look up here towards the hill, they are coming,
let us go and meet them.

MRS. DARLINGTON. No, my dear, father is so nervous, let us wait.

[HELEN *waives her handkerchief.*]

Mrs. Darlington. I cannot tell which of those two young men, Fred. is.

Helen. O, I can—this one, the tall one, O no ! the short one. I don't know myself, it is so long since we have seen our Fred.

[*Enter* Captain, Fred., Pierre *and* Jonathan, *by C. D. in F.*]

Captain. Lucy my dear, Helen—here is our son, our long absent love, your brother Fred.

[Helen *and* Mrs. Darlington *embracing* Pierre, *in mistake for* Frederick.]

Captain. Why dear, this is not Fred, this is Mr. Pierre Livingston.

[Mrs. Darlington *and* Helen *rush to* Fred. *embracing and kissing him.*]

Captain. Ladies; Mr. Pierre Livingston.

Jonathan. (*Rushing towards the ladies.*) Ladies, my name is Jonathan Skinner, esq., from Vermont.

[Helen *and* Mrs. Darlingtgn *bow.*]

Jonathan. Captain, why don't you say at once—you might as well say, your intended son-in-law.

Helen. (*Aside.*) What a gallant.

Captain. Jonathan, you are so hasty in all your ways.

Jonathan. (*Pointing towards* Helen.) O Jehosophat, ain't she plump. O look at her feet, wall now I like Dolly Pimpkins's better, because they are four times bigger. Just look at her eyes, they look like our huckleberries, yum, yum, ain't they blue.

Mrs. Darlington. Dear Fred., you are changed to be sure. When you left home you were a mere lad, and now you are quite a man. How well you look, I am so proud of you.

Helen. O how rejoiced I am to have once more a brother's protection.

Fred. Mother, dear Helen,—my heart is overcome with joy, to be with you once more. "O ! home, sweet home." Mother, this is my friend, he has been with me constantly for three years, and is more like a brother than a stranger. He was formerly from these parts.

Mrs. Darlington. Indeed, I must then have known your parents.

Pierre. No doubt. (*Aside*) I will not go any farther on this subject. I am honored to be among my friends. (*Aside, looking towards* Helen.) What a beautiful girl.

HELEN. Mother let me go to Walter's mother, and tell her of the good news of Fred's return.

MRS. DARLINGTON. No, dear Helen, I will have Fred. go with me to her house, and introduce him to her. Mr. Livingston will join us.

PIERRE. I am somewhat fatigued. (*Aside.*) Some excuse to remain.

MRS. DARLINGTON. Get everything in readiness for our holiday dinner.

CAPTAIN. Lucy, I suppose I am of no account any more. You don't ask me to go. All right, the time will come again.

MRS. DARLINGTON. O, I don't forget you altogether; come, dear, go with us. Helen, entertain Mr. Livingston while we are gone, it will not be long.

HELEN. Don't be long; I will have everything prepared by your return.

MRS. DARLINGTON. In one hour we will return. (MRS. DARLINGTON, CAPTAIN *and* FRED. *going towards door in the act of leaving.*)

JONATHAN. Well, I guess I'm nobody. (*Going towards* PIERRE.) I say, traveling mate, you might as well go with your friends. I'm that girl's choice. (*Going towards* HELEN, *and trying to pinch her cheek.*) Aint I your deary? Why look at my long, beautiful hair, this fellow had the gouting fever, all his hair is short and stiff as corn cobs.

MRS. DARLINGTON. Jonathan, come with us, Mr. Pierre will remain with Helen.

JONATHAN. You can't fool this 'ere boy, not if the Court knows herself, and she thinks she does. I am here, and this old pumpkinhead can't euchre me out of this girl. I hold the right and left bower and have got the joker up my sleeve.

MRS. DARLINGTON. Come with us, Jonathan.

JONATHAN. Well, I see the old woman has taken a fancy to me. I'm going to be the next Pa here, and cut the old Captain out.

CAPTAIN. What did you say?

JONATHAN. O, don't mind me, old Captain; only a little joke, see.

[MRS. DARLINGTON, CAPTAIN, FRED. *and* JONATHAN *exit by C. D. in F. to the right.*]

JONATHAN. (*Looking around.*) I say, girl. (*Throwing kisses at her.*) .

HELEN. Ring the bell.

[AGNES *enters by D. in F. left.*]

3*

HELEN.   Agnes, prepare everything for dinner.   Mother and father will soon return; we expect some guests to-day.
AGNES.   Miss Helen, all will be ready in due time.
AGNES.   (*Aside.*)   I don't like the looks of this man.

[*Exit by C. D. left.*]

PIERRE.   (*Coming towards* HELEN.)   How pleasantly you are situated here—quite romantic.
HELEN.   Yes, but——
PIERRE.   You are not contented I see?
HELEN.   Even on this joyful day I feel melancholy.
PIERRE.   If I may be inquisitive, what is the cause?
HELEN.   I cannot explain.
PIERRE.   Love, no doubt.
HELEN.   (*Blushing, turning away her head.*)   O! no, sir.
PIERRE.   As far as my experience goes, if you young girls are once in love nothing pleases them only the one they love.
HELEN.   Sir, let us change our conversation to some other subject. You have been acquainted with my brother for some time, and no doubt a bosom companion in part of his adventures.
PIERRE.   I certainly have, but it would not be pleasant for a young lady to listen to them.
HELEN.   The time seems so long that mother stays away.   Mr. Livingston, you will find some interesting books in the library.   (*Points towards the left.*)   You will entertain yourself, as I have to attend to some domestic duties.
PIERRE.   O, don't leave me!   (*Attempts to encircle her with his arm.*)
HELEN.   Sir, as a friend of my brother's I respect you, but remember, sir, I am alone and a defenceless girl.
PIERRE.   O, sweet creature!   The moment I entered your house those bright eyes, your sweet countenance, your lovely figure, all bewitched me, my heart commenced to beat for you.   I,—I cannot speak, I dare not.   Helen, I love you.   Give me but one kiss from those rosy lips.
HELEN.   (*Moving away from* PIERRE, *seems agitated.*)   Sir! leave this house at once.   I will call for assistance.   How can you thus insult me under my parents' roof.
PIERRE.   Silence—some one is coming.

[*Enter* MRS. DARLINGTON, FRED., CAPTAIN, MRS. OSGOOD *and* JONATHAN, *by C. D. F.*]

HELEN.   (*Running towards her mother.*)   O, dear mother, how glad I am you have returned. Mrs. Osgood, you are welcome. We are overjoyed with the return of my brother. O, I look for the day when we will be blessed with the return of our Walter.

MRS. OSGOOD. I am very happy on your account, my dear. Have patience, and all will come right.

HELEN. With the blessing of Heaven, I trust in God. (HELEN *going to her mother.*) I don't like this man Livingston.

MRS. DARLINGTON. And what reason have you for saying so?

HELEN. I cannot explain now, but let father induce Fred. to take Mr. Livingston to some other house to stay.

MRS. DARLINGTON. There must be something wrong, otherwise you would not speak thus.

[*Bell rings for dinner.*]

HELEN. Mother, as I promised before you left, all is ready as you ordered.

MRS. DARLINGTON. Come Mrs. Osgood, come gentlemen, this way, (*moving toward left of stage,*) to the dining hall, (*3 E. L.*)

[*Exeunt, all except* PIERRE *and* CAPTAIN.]

CAPTAIN. From the conversation I have had with Fred. I learn you have always acted towards him, not only as a friend, but like a brother. Any assistance I can render you will be a pleasure to me.

PIERRE. I am under many obligations to you, and I am proud to have your friendship, and to have the honor of being among your noble family.

CAPTAIN. You will tell me of your parents, and the history of your early life?

PIERRE. There is a secret connected with that, but as you are my benefactor, how could I withhold it from you.

CAPTAIN. Sir! you are a gentleman, and a man of honor.

PIERRE. I am your most obedient—

CAPTAIN. Well tell me, our time is short, our friends are waiting for us at dinner.

PIERRE. How sad I feel to speak of those once so dear to me. I have but a faint recollection of them, but I will, as far as my recollection serves me, tell you all, as I consider you, sir, now as my protector, my friend. I was born in a small town in New England, and while quite young my parents moved to Providence, and there my father obtained a situation as first book-keeper in some banking house, the name I do not recollect. When I attained the age of fifteen my mother died, and left me under the care of our good old housekeeper Mrs. Blanchard, a good old soul. A month after the death of my poor dear mother my father left his home, and I was left in the care of Mrs. Blanchard, and since that sorrowful day I have never heard of him. I always was of a roving disposition, and unknown to my guardian, I left home, and wandered from place to place with hopes of finding my father, but all in vain, and then at last I resorted to gambling, and from that you, and you alone, saved me. As to our good old housekeeper, I have learned since my absence she has gone to a better place—and now, sir, you have all that I know of my early life.

CAPTAIN. This is sad indeed, may the day soon arrive when you will once more see your father. You are young, the world is open before you, and I will consider it a duty on my part to take your father's place.

PIERRE. Oh sir! how thankful I am to you, and I will always try to merit your friendship and protection.

CAPTAIN. Come let us join our friends now, and on some future occasion we will speak again on this subject.

[CAPTAIN *and* PIERRE *move towards dining hall, 3 L. E.*]

PIERRE. (*Aside.*) Could I but gain the Captain's confidence, and his permission to make Helen, this beautiful girl, my wife, I would try to gain her affections.

[*Exit 3 L. E.*]

[MRS. OSGOOD *enters 3rd L. E.*]

MRS. OSGOOD. I could not enjoy my dinner, or anything else. O, how anxious I do feel to hear some news from Walter. The steamer has arrived safe in Liverpool, about twelve days ago, but I know Walter has always been so slow in his correspondence. (*The clock strikes two.*) Why how fast the forenoon has passed.

[*Enter Helen from 3rd L. E.*]

MRS. OSGOOD. (*Going towards Helen.*) Helen, my dear, I am so glad to see you, it did not take you long for your dinner.

HELEN. My dear Mrs. Osgood, father and mother have gone out to spend the day, I will be so lonely at home, you stay with me and spend the afternoon with me.

MRS. OSGOOD. You are so kind, I will do so.

[HELEN *takes chair and sits down.*]

HELEN. I had a pleasant dream last night, but alas, it was but a dream.

MRS. OSGOOD. Tell me your dream.

HELEN. That we received a letter and good news from Walter

MRS. OSGOOD. I thought before you came it must be time for us to receive a letter.

HELEN. Mrs. Osgood, it is but a short distance, I will go the post-office, and oh! how fortunate I would consider myself to bring you a letter, and my dream may turn out to be a reality.

MRS. OSGOOD. Go dear Helen, and may God be your guide.

HELEN. I will not be long, adieu.

[Exit C. D. F.]

MRS. OSGOOD. What a darling girl. O, Walter, may you be blessed in your undertakings, that you may be enabled at one day to call Helen your own dear wife—Some one is approaching!

[Enter PIERRE from 3rd L. E.]

PIERRE. I beg pardon for the intrusion.

MRS. OSGOOD. *(Aside.)* What means this?

PIERRE. I thought to inquire if you had received any news from your son Walter.

MRS. OSGOOD. I thank you kindly sir, for the interest you take in the welfare of my son.

PIERRE. *(Aside.)* She don't suspect my errand. Madam I can imagine a mother's feelings in being separated from her only child, and one who, I have heard, was so kind and affectionate to you.

MRS. OSGOOD. Yes sir, he is a noble son, and worthy of any one's love, and the love of Helen Darlington.

PIERRE. Has Miss Helen been here within the last half hour? She left the hall so suddenly.

MRS. OSGOOD. Yes!—no! no!

PIERRE. You mean yes, or no?

[JONATHAN enters from C. D. F.]

JONATHAN. *(Aside.)* By Jove, here is that monkey again. After my girl, no doubt. He'll not go out of my sight. I say, you young sprout, what are you after now? Look here old woman, I'm here, I can take care of the house. You are a widow and need protection, and I am the protector of widows and pretty orphans.

MRS. OSGOOD. I am obliged for your kind consideration.

PIERRE. *(Aside.)* This cursed fool will spoil my game.

JONATHAN. I say young fellow, the air is fresh, and you look like some pure air will do you good. This is what we call in Vermont a polite invitation to vamoose and git.

MRS. OSGOOD. Miss Helen was here a few moments ago, but she left for the post-office. She is expecting some letters.

JONATHAN. That's so, old woman, she expected three or four from me.

PIERRE. Silence, fool.

JONATHAN. Did you say fool, well if I'm a fool, you are a jackass, and they know less. (*Aside.*) That joker ain't up my sleeve for nothing.

MRS. OSGOOD. I understand your intentions, Mr. Pierre Livingston, very well.

JONATHAN. (*Going towards the door and looking for* HELEN.) Here she comes, and how sweet she looks. By Jove she's a stunner.

[*Enter* HELEN, *C. D. in F.*]

HELEN. (*Aside.*) Pierre here. (*Running towards Mrs. Osgood.*) O dear Mrs. Osgood, my dream is a reality. I have two letters, one for you and one for me. (*Kisses the letters.*)

MRS. OSGOOD. You are an angel from Heaven, to bring me news from my dear son.

PIERRE. (*Aside.*) I guess I can be spared here just now. Ladies, I will take my leave.

JONATHAN. I say, my boy, you'll take nothing from this house, no leaves or anything else; for I am the widow's protector.

HELEN. (*Aside.*) I wish he had not come here.

JONATHAN. Did you get my letters, I did not direct them, I thought if I did some other gal might get them.

MRS. OSGOOD. Gentlemen, I will be pleased to see you soon again.

JONATHAN. You don't mean this pumpkin head to come again, if you do why I shall stay away, now then, how would you like that. You know he wants to cut me out, but he can't. (*Commences to cry aloud, takes a large red handkerchief from his pocket.*)

PIERRE. Ladies, your most obedient. (*Exit C. D. F.*)

JONATHAN. By Jove, I'll follow him, and if I get him in a dark place I'll blow his old pudding head off his shoulders, I will as sure as my name is Jonathan Skinner. I won't be long.

[*Exit C. D. in F.*]

HELEN. How relieved I feel when this man is out of my sight.

MRS. OSGOOD. Helen, I don't like this man Pierre Livingston.

HELEN. Neither do I.

[MRS. OSGOOD *and* HELEN *each take a chair and sit close together.*]

HELEN. My letter I have read, I could not wait to take it home. You know, Mrs. Osgood, lovers always have some secrets.

MRS. OSGOOD. To be sure.

[HELEN *opens letter and reads it to* MRS. OSGOOD.]

" *My Dear Mother* :—After a short and pleasant journey, I reached
" Liverpool in safety yesterday. I trust you and dear Helen will enjoy
" good health. I am blessed with that privilege, but low-spirited, to
" think how far I am separated from those so dear to me. My prayers
" are that our separation shall only be but for a short duration. My
" prospects for the future seem bright to me, and with these hopes I
" keep up spirits. I will always remember my promise to return and
" be worthy of your love and affection. Home, ever so humble, is bet-
" ter than to live in palaces abroad and away from those you so dearly
" love.

" Dear mother, I pass many sleepless nights in thinking of you, and
" of her I adore. In my dreams I see thee both before me, but when
" I awake, alas! I find it but a dream. Mother, give me your daily
" blessing, the same as when I was at home, and pray for my safe
" return—and then our home will be as a paradise to me. Now be
" blessed, and remember, your son,

WALTER.

" P. S.—As soon as I reach my destination I will write again. I
" have written to Helen. Adieu.

WALTER."

HELEN. Now, Mrs. Osgood, this is good news.

MRS. OSGOOD. Good news; why I am so happy. Blessed boy.

HELEN. My parents will be overjoyed. No doubt they have returned by this time. I will go and see.

MRS. OSGOOD. Do so, I will follow you.

[*Exeunt* HELEN *and* MRS. OSGOOD *by C. D. in F.*]

END OF ACT III.

ACT IV.

SCENE I.—PALACE SQUARE AT ST. PETERSBURG. *Snowing. In back-ground a large wall representing the Palace wall. Two Sentinels walking in front. Two large lamps at entrance of Palace. Door in centre of flat.*

[*Enter* WALTER *from S. E. L.*]

WALTER. (*In deep meditation.*) I hope my letters have reached home, because I know how anxious my dear mother was to hear from me, and as to Helen, no doubt she will read my letter over and over again, and know of my safe arrival at Liverpool. O! home, sweet home! will I ever see thee again, fool that I am. Remember the words of Captain Darlington:—" Courage my boy, there is no such word as fail." I trust in God that I may gain my object. No dear Mother at my side. No Helen to look at her bright eyes like stars in heaven! No words of consolation; but my future hopes are like glittering diamonds. How strange the people do look here in St. Petersburg, and so many gens d'armes, as they call them. They look at me as though I was a spy or something of the kind. I fear nothing. I am a true American. There is no such word with us as fear. I must try to find a comfortable home to stay at. "Home," did I say? Where are you, away, far away. I wish I could only find some Americans, there are many here I am told.

[*A gentleman about fifty years of age,* EDWARD SINGLETON, *approaches from upper entrance.* WALTER *goes toward him.*]

WALTER. Sir! I beg your pardon, but as I am a stranger here would you please direct me to a good hotel ?

EDWARD. It will please me to give you any information possible. A stranger, and on such a stormy day as this, I consider it a duty.

WALTER. I am under many obligations, sir.

EDWARD. From what part of the world do you come ?

WALTER. From blessed America.

EDWARD. (*Joyfully running towards* WALTER.) Give me your hand sir ; from America did you say—from what part of America ?

WALTER. From Providence, Rhode Island.

EDWARD. (*Aside.*) My once sweet home.

WALTER. What did you say? Home, from what home?

EDWARD. I said, sir, you were so far away from your home.

WALTER. I am, but with hopes soon to return again.

EDWARD. And are you traveling for pleasure or on business.

WALTER. This, sir, I will explain on some future occasion.

EDWARD. O! do tell me, I am so interested in your behalf as an American. If I can be of any service to you, name it, and I am your most obedient.

WALTER. I am obliged to you for your kind consideration, and hope the day may be not long distant when I can return to you the kind feelings you bear towards me.

EDWARD. You can stay at my lodgings while here, it will be pleasant for both of us. I want you to tell me all the news you can from your home.

WALTER. Did you say home, that word is so sweet to me? Why, are you from America?

EDWARD. Yes sir, and I am proud to be an American.

WALTER. You may well say proud. We may be so of that blessed land. Are the customs and ways here much different from ours?

EDWARD. Altogether different, you may say, in every way, the customs, the people, and everything else. But tell me, what is your name?

WALTER. I will tell you my name. My name, sir, is Walter Osgood.

EDWARD. Great Heaven, the son of my old friend Osgood. (*Rushes to* WALTER *and embraces him.*) May God bless you my boy. I will be your protector and adviser.

WALTER. My hopes are realized. I said my future was bright. How glad I am to meet a friend of my father's in a distant land.

EDWARD. When you have been here a short time you will like the country better. You will become familiar with the customs, and as to the gensd'armes, if they look with suspicion on you—why they think every stranger is a spy, and may have come here for some purpose against the Government—but they have great faith in Americans here.

WALTER. I hope to be contented while here, and the more so to be with you; but tell me your name, and your business here? How did you come to make this country your home?

EDWARD. Well, listen. Some twelve years ago, I left Providence. In those days I was engaged as head clerk at the Banking house of Emory Dorman & Co. Through misfortunes and financial embarrassments—I cannot go on. The recollection of those days makes my blood run cold through my veins.

4

WALTER.   O! do go on, we are now and forever sworn confidential friends.

EDWARD.   I have committed a great crime.   (*Becomes embarrassed in manner.*)   Yes, I have committed a forgery.   My wife died some time before, with shame and remorse I resolved to leave my once happy home.   O God, when I think of that day!   I had a son then about the age of fifteen, and left him in care of my old housekeeper for her to attend to his education ; but alas, I have had no tidings from them, as they did not know what direction I would take.   If I could only once more behold my only child, to press him to his father's bosom—O! I cannot go on any further with my story.

WALTER.   But you did not tell me your name.

EDWARD.   Here I have adopted the name of Edward Singleton, not to disgrace the name my father bore, but to you and you alone I will reveal my name ; my name is—is André Livingston.

WALTER.   (*Rushing towards Edward and embracing him*)   You, then, the father of Pierre Livingston, my school companion?   O, God, this is too much!

EDWARD.   Have you been with my son before your departure?

WALTER.   Nothing would afford me more pleasure than to inform you in regard to Pierre; but I unfortunately cannot give you any information of him of late years.   When quite a boy he left home.   I well recollect your housekeeper, her name was Mrs. Blanchard.

EDWARD.   Go on ; go on.

WALTER.   She died; and as to Pierre, we have never heard from him since.

EDWARD.   And could you recollect what has become of the House of Emory Dorman & Co.

WALTER.   Some few years ago Emory Dorman died, and the firm has since changed its name, but I do not recollect to what.   Emory Dorman left a large fortune.   Among his papers was a document in which he expressed his desire that any employé who had ever committed an error of any kind should be forgiven and free from all prosecution in the country, and if abroad might return in safety.

EDWARD.   Thank God, I am a free man!   Pierre, your father will and must find you.   Walter, this news makes me feel twenty years younger.

WALTER.   When I write I will inform my mother of our happy meeting.   How happy she will be to know that I have met a friend of our family.

EDWARD.   Do so.   But let us go to our lodgings, you must be fatigued.

[*Exeunt* EDWARD *and* WALTER, *S. E. L.*]

CORRUNE. Aldro, how is it the Emperor did not leave the palace to-day.

ALDRO. The stormy weather is no doubt the cause.

CORRUNE. Take a nap, Aldro. Lay down, you look sleepy.

[ALDRO *lays down in front of gate and sleeps.*]

CORRUNE. Now is my chance to take a drink, the fool sleeps. (*Takes a bottle from his pocket and drinks freely.*) Well that does a soul good. How sleepy it makes me feel. Let me take another drink. (*Drinks again and lies down and falls asleep.*)

[*Enter* WALTER *from S. E. L.*]

WALTER. Why, if these are fair samples of Russian soldiers, God help the country in time of war. I had better leave, this is no place for me. I am on the wrong route.

[*Exit by S. E. R.*]

[*Enter* COUNT ABREGE, *3 E. R.*]

COUNT. This is a stormy day. On such a day as this, I always take the route by the Palace to avoid the long hills to my chateau. But what do I see, both sentinels asleep; this is a dreadful affair; they shall be court-martialed forthwith. I will not disturb them, but will go to my chateau and send a guard to arrest them.

[*Dropping a large wallet from under his cloak, exit 3 E. L.*]

[*Enter* WALTER, *3 E. R., stumbles over the wallet.*]

WALTER. What have we here. (*Opens the wallet.*) A large amount of money and sealed documents. What name is this on the wallet,— "Count Abrege, Russian Army." No doubt this must be his Palace. I will enter, these fellows are asleep, but how will I gain admittance ; this must be returned to the rightful owner. (*Goes to gate and removes the bars, and enters the Palace saying:—*) Honesty is always reward-ed in return by some act of kindness. As poor as I am, and destitute of funds, remember, let no temptation lead me from the path of virtue. And now for the Count. (*Enters.*)

[*Immediately a shot is heard and bell rung. Sentinels awaken.*]

ALDRO. Corrune, something is wrong, the bars have been removed. O dear! O dear! we will be shot.

CORRUNE. No one has seen us asleep.

ALDRO. That is more than you know.

[*A guard speaking loudly from within* :—" *You are my prisoner, you are a spy.*"]

[*Enter* WALTER *and* GUARD *from inside of Palace.*]

GUARD.   Corrune and Aldro, take your prisoner to the Guard House.

WALTER.   I am no spy, no traitor, I wanted to restore something that I found to the Count Abrege.

GUARD.   The Count is at his chateau.   Away with him.

[CORRUNE *taking* WALTER *prisoner.   Exit by 3 E. L.*]

ALDRO.   This fellow has planned some plot, and if he has he will find St. Petersburgh a pretty hard place.   (*Looking towards 3 E. L.*]

[CORRUNE *enters from 3 E. L.*]

CORRUNE.   This fellow is no spy that I locked up just now.   He is a gentleman, whoever he may be.

ALDRO.   You cannot tell by appearances now-a-days.

[*Enter* EDWARD SINGLETON *from S. E. R.*]

EDWARD.   I have heard that some one has been arrested as a spy, could you give me his description?

CORRUNE.   We can give no description to any one, you can get it at the head-quarters, or at the bureau of police.   He is safe where the dogs cannot bite him.

EDWARD.   No doubt this must be Walter.   If I can but prove his innocence, and get him released.

[*The bell rings.*]

CORRUNE.   You will excuse me, my duty calls me; I have to leave. Come, Aldro.

[*Exeunt* CORRUNE *and* ALDRO, *S. E. L.*]

EDWARD.   I must and shall release him if it cost my life.

[*Exit by S. E. R.*]

[BOREISO *and* CALENDO *enter from S. E. L.*]

BOREISO.   This prisoner brought to the guard-house, for shooting at the guard at the palace, is a foreigner.

CALENDO.   Yes, he is an American.

BOREISO.   Corrune has told me he acted so strangely on his way to the guard-house, and wanted to know what prison our life convicts are confined in. There must be some secret connected with this American.

CALENDO. There is no doubt this fellow will be transfered from the guard-house to the Bastile, and then we will have him under our charge. We will allow him no privileges, and treat him as we do our own prisoners ; if we did not, you know the consequence.

BORIESO. I have been connected with the prison too long not to know my duty.

CALENDO. These Americans are smart fellows, and no doubt he wanted to learn something of our secret of making Russian iron, and then if successful would make a fortune in his own country, if he were ever to reach there again.

[BOREISO *looking towards S. E. L.*]

BOREISO. Here comes the guard, no doubt, as you said, to transfer the prisoner to the Bastile.

[*Officer and five guards enter in charge of* WALTER *from S. E. L.*]

REMO. (*Handing a paper to* CALENDO.) By order of the magistrate, I hand this prisoner over to you to be transfered to the Bastile until further orders, and allow no one to visit him without a written permission from the magistrate.

CALENDO. (*Tipping his hat.*) We will obey your orders.

[*Guards leave by S. E. L.*]

WALTER. (*To guards.*) From your long and constant duty with prisoners no doubt your hearts lack sympathy, and therefore become cold as stone ; yet there must be one spark of humanity within you. Now, listen to me ; as God is my judge I am no spy, nor have I any criminal intention, and my errand to the palace was an honest one.

CALENDO. You are mistaken, sir; our feelings are always with the unfortunate, but we must do our duty. The time is up and we will now conduct you to the Bastile.

WALTER. Dear mother, could you but look upon me now, a prisoner in a strange land—but I'll be brave, and I know that honesty will always be rewarded.

CALENDO. (*To* WALTER.) Follow me.

[BOREISO *rear of* WALTER.]

4*

SCENE II.—NARROW STAGE, REPRESENTING FRONT OF A PRISON. *Two doors in flat, right and left. The left door to have a wicket.*

[CALENDO *and* BOREISO *enter from R. D. in flat.*]

CALENDO.   Our hero is safe in his lodgings.

BOREISO.   I tell you once more, this fellow has seen better days and is no criminal.

CALENDO.   Time will tell, Boreiso ; now go your rounds, and see that everything is right.

[BOREISO *exit, R. D. in flat.*]

CALENDO.   I hope the poor fellow can prove his innocence, so that he can be released.

[BOREISO *enters from R. D. in flat.*]

BOREISO.   Our young American prisoner wants to speak to you.

CALENDO.   Open his cell and bring him here.

[BOREISO *exit by R. D.*]

CALENDO.   According to the rules of the Bastile I ought not to do so, but I have a son myself, and who knows in what trouble he may get himself some day.

[BOREISO *enters by R. D. with* WALTER, *who is dressed in striped clothing, and looking pale.*]

WALTER.   I have wronged you both, when I said you had no feelings and your hearts were like stone. Thanks to Heaven I am mistaken. I wish to speak a few words to you, only.

CALENDO.   Boreiso, go to the cells of the life convicts and see if everything is right.

[BOREISO *exit R. D.*]

CALENDO.   (*To* WALTER.)   Now proceed, I will listen.

WALTER.   How long have you been a guard in this prison.

CALENDO.   Some years, but it is a most dreadful life, and believe me, if I could find some other occupation, I'd say good-bye to prison life, but what can I do, I have no means, I am very poor.

WALTER.   You know the charge that I am here for, but I wanted to act as an honest man should, and in a moment of passion I fired my pistol. But I only fired into the air, and with no intention to harm any one. I wanted to restore the wallet, I found in front of the Palace, to Count Abrege.

CALENDO. Well, did you return it?

WALTER. No, but I will, as soon as an interview is allowed me with the Count.

CALENDO. He is a noble soul, and no doubt will have you released.

WALTER. O, I thank you, you have a noble heart. I have a great favor to ask of you, and I swear to you that if I am released, I will well reward you if you get me, in writing, the directions of how Russian iron is made in this prison.

CALENDO. This is impossible, if I would a long imprisonment would follow and then what should become of my family.

WALTER. But not until I am ready to leave this country for my home in America, and then if you will, I swear it will remain a secret with me. I swear never to reveal it to any one.

CALENDO. When you are released inform me where I can meet you alone. I will hand you then the necessary information, but remember the reward and your oath.

WALTER. I swear it.___

[BOREISO *enters from R. D. in flat.*]

BOREISO. Well, what was it the fellow wanted?

CALENDO. He said he felt so lonely and wanted an English book.

BOREISO. We have no library here for convicts.

CALENDO. You have no feeling for any one. He is no convict, he is only here on a petty charge.

[*A knock is heard at the L. D. prison.*]

BOREISO. (*Opens wicket in gate.*) Who is there?

EDWARD. (*From without.*) I have a permit to see a friend of mine in this prison.

BOREISO. Let me see it.

[EDWARD *hands paper through wicket.*]

BOREISO. Calendo, come here, is this all right?

CALENDO. All right, let him pass.

[*Door opens and* EDWARD *enters.*]

CALENDO. Boreiso, search him, and see that he has nothing contrary to the prison rules.

BOREISO. (*Searches* EDWARD.) All right. What is the prisoner's name?

EDWARD. He is a young American, and is charged with attempting to shoot a guard.

CALENDO. I cannot pass you to his cell, but I'll bring him here, and your interview must be in my presence, according to the rules of the prison.

EDWARD. Thank you. I have no secrets, and would not do any-thing that is contrary to your rules.

CALENDO. I will bring in the prisoner.

[*Exit by R. D.*]

EDWARD. How sad I feel to meet my friend in such a horrible place.

[CALENDO *and* WALTER *enter from R. D.*]

WALTER. O, Edward, you have come, Could you but know my feelings away from home, and you my only friend here.

EDWARD. Be a man; keep courage; I will do all I can to have an interview with Count Abrege, who is the only gentleman who can help me to get you released.

WALTER. Great God! that name; it is the Count then that can through his influence obtain my release It was the Count's wallet I found with a large amount of money and papers, and it was to his palace I thought I had gone to restore his wallet, and the inside guard refused to allow me to pass; it was then I fired, but did not intend to kill the guard.

EDWARD. I am sure Walter, you will be released, as you have acted as an honest man. I will not lose any time and shall go forthwith.

CALENDO. (*To Edward.*) Your time is up and five minutes over.

EDWARD. I thank you for your indulgence.

WALTER Go, Edward, and may God speed your way.

EDWARD. It will not be long before I return with the documents for your release. (EDWARD *embracing* WALTER.) Farewell.

[EDWARD *exit by L. D.*]

[*Bell rings.*]

CALENDO. This is the relief bell, the other guards come on duty now, and I will conduct you to your cell.

[CALENDO *and* WALTER *exit by R. D.*]

[Two prison guards enter from L. D.]

FIRST GUARD   I met Count Abrege on horse-back near the bridge.

SECOND GUARD.   He is so kind to the prisoners.   He often comes here and gives them words of consolation.

[A knock is heard from without on L. D.]

FIRST GUARD.   Open the wicket and see who it is.

SECOND GUARD.   It is the Count and some stranger.

FIRST GUARD.   Open the door.

*[*COUNT *and* EDWARD *enter.]*

[Both guards bow.]

FIRST GUARD.   Your humble servant, what can I do for your Excellency?

COUNT.   I came here as usual to comfort the unfortunate ones, and also to see a young American.   I would like to speak to him.

FIRST GUARD.   Will it please your Excellency to see him now?

COUNT.   Not just now, you can both retire and return in a half hour.

[Both guards bow and exit by R. D.]

EDWARD.   I beg pardon sir, but as I was on my way to your chateau I met you on the road, and from your description, I thought I had the honor of meeting your Excellency, Count Abrege.

COUNT.   Yes sir, I am Count Abrege—and can I be of any service to you?

EDWARD.   You can, sir; and after you have listened to me no doubt your kind and noble heart will at once release one from this prison who is innocent of a grave charge.

COUNT.   Well, sir, go on, and tell me.

EDWARD.   A young American, unacquainted with the customs of this country, entered the gates of the palace, thinking you resided there, to restore to you a wallet, marked with your name, he found in front of the palace.   Admittance was refused him, he fired a pistol, with no malicious intent, and for that he is in this prison, awaiting his sentence.

COUNT.   Brave fellow, his honesty shall be well rewarded; and as to his release, follow me, and we will see to it at once.

EDWARD.   O, sir, accept many thanks, and the blessings of his old mother, now so far away from him.

[The two guards enter from R. D.]

FIRST GUARD. Will your Excellency have an interview with the young American ?

COUNT. Bring him in.

[*Two guards exit by. R. D.*]

EDWARD. O, sir, how grateful this young man will be to his bene-factor.

[*Two guards enter with* WALTER *by R. D.* WALTER *bows.*]

COUNT. Your friend has told me all, and your honesty will be re-warded, and I will obtain your release forthwith. Your pardon I will send to you by your friend, and he is indeed your friend.

WALTER. Sir, I am overcome with emotions of gratitude, and when once again in my native land, I shall often think of you, and pray that God may spare the friend of the unfortunate. Your wallet, sir, was taken from me by the Commissioner of Police, and from him you can get it.

COUNT. You will be rewarded as your honesty deserves.—(*To* ED-WARD.) You follow me.—(*To* WALTER.) It will not be long before your friend will return with your pardon.

WALTER. May heaven bless you.

[COUNT *and* EDWARD *exit by L. D.*]

FIRST GUARD, My relief will soon be here. I will conduct you to your cell, and I hope you will soon leave this prison.

WALTER. You are so kind.

[*Bell rings.*]

[CALENDO *and* BOREISO *enter.*]

CALENDO. You can go now, guard ; I will bring the prisoner to his cell.

[*Guards exit by L. D.*]

BOREISO. I will go and do my rounds, and soon return.

[*Knock at the door.*]

CALENDO. (*Looking through the wicket.*) Who is there ?

EDWARD. I am the friend of your American prisoner, and I have his pardon.

WALTER. O, God, I hear his voice.

[CALENDO *opens the door.*]

[EDWARD, *handing a large paper with red seal.* CALENDO *looking over paper.*]

CALENDO. This is all right, you are pardoned.

WALTER. (*Running towards* EDWARD *and embracing him.*) You are a true *Damon.*

EDWARD. The Count has sent you a large amount of bank notes, which were in the wallet that you found, as your reward ; and he sends his blessings to you, and hopes for your future welfare. I must look to my horse outside, as I came here in post haste. I will return in a few moments. Now, arrange yourself for your departure from this gloomy place. (*Handing Walter a paper package.*)

WALTER. Don't be long as I'm anxious for your return.

[EDWARD *exit by L. D.*]

CALENDO. How pleased I am that you are free, and the promise I made to you I have kept. Here is the document which contains the secret ; but remember your oath.

WALTER. I swear it ! (*Opening the package and giving him some notes.*)

CALENDO. You have kept your word as a gentleman.

[EDWARD *enters from L. D.*]

EDWARD. I forgot to tell you that my errand boy gave me a letter for you, and it comes from America. (*Handing* WALTER *a letter.*)

WALTER. It is from home ! (*Opening in haste, and reading it over and over.*)

WALTER. All good news—they are all well, in good hopes for my safe return, and Helen's long lost brother is found. And such good news for you also ; Pierre Livingston, your son, has returned with Frederick Darlington.

EDWARD. O, what a day of joy for me. Now we will both return to America.

WALTER. That is the very proposition I was going to make. I have plenty of means, I will share with you.

EDWARD. No, my son, in the long absence from my home I have accumulated quite a handsome fortune, and part of that is at your command.

WALTER. Then at once let us prepare for our journey to our happy home.

EDWARD. So said, so done ; let us go. May God be our guide.

(*Exeunt* WALTER *and* EDWARD *by L. D.*)

ACT V.

SCENE I.—SAME SCENE AS FIRST SCENE IN THIRD ACT. *In addition a table with refreshments and bouquets of flowers. Door in centre of flat, two windows on each side of door.*

[*Enter* CAPTAIN DARLINGTON, *3 E. L.*]

CAPTAIN. This day, twenty-five years ago, I married my dear Lucy, and we hope to have a pleasant day to celebrate our silver wedding. But my dear Helen's joy will not be complete; she has had no news of late from her Walter. Some one is coming.

[*Enter* MRS. OSGOOD, *C. D. in F.*]

MRS. OSGOOD. Good morning, Captain; how is your wife and dear Helen?

CAPTAIN. I am so glad to see you. How pleased my wife and Helen will be to have you among us at our celebration.

MRS. OSGOOD. I received your kind invitation, and consider it a high honor to be one of your guests. Where is Helen? The steamer arrived yesterday at New York from Europe, and we may get some news to-day.

CAPTAIN. This would be pleasant,—it would rejoice our Helen so much. She will be here soon. She always takes a walk in the garden every morning of late. She likes to be by herself. She always seems in deep meditation.

MRS. OSGOOD. (*Going to window L.*) Captain, she is coming.

[*Enter* HELEN, *3 E. L.*]

HELEN. I am delighted to see you. How well you do look.

MRS. OSGOOD. I thank you, dear Helen. You are looking well. The steamer arrived yesterday, let us hope for some good news from Walter. It is now over six weeks since he wrote.

HELEN. How the time passes, but I am not sorry, for this will bring back my dear Walter so much sooner.

MRS. OSGOOD.—Patience, dear, and all will come right. I know it will.

CAPTAIN. Helen, my dear, you must be cheerful this day, otherwise our féte would not be complete, and then your mother would be so down-hearted to see you low spirited.

HELEN. Father, to please you and mother I would do almost anything.

CAPTAIN. You are a good girl, and we are proud of you.

MRS. OSGOOD. O, I know Helen, you will do all you can to make this a pleasant affair.

HELEN. Mrs. Osgood, and father, come near to me, I have something to tell you.

[CAPTAIN *and* MRS. OSGOOD *approach Helen.*]

HELEN. Last night, as I was walking through the garden in the beautiful moonlight, I was thinking of my dear Walter's safe return, and at that moment what do you think ?

MRS. OSGOOD. And what dear ?

HELEN. A star from Heaven shot through the sky, and my dear mother always said if you wished for anything at that time it was sure to come. Is not that so father ?

MRS. OSGOOD. We old folks have very funny notions. I only hope it may turn out to be a good omen.

CAPTAIN. When you said old folks, did you include my Lucy ? No indeed, she feels as young as twenty-five years ago, the day I married her.

MRS. OSGOOD. You are a good husband. My dear departed husband was just like you.

HELEN. Where is mother ?

CAPTAIN. She is no doubt making her toilet for to-day's celebraion. Helen, you have no doubt invited all your friends ?

HELEN. Why, on such an occasion as this, I would not forget my friends. I have prepared, for you and mother, two most beautiful bouquets of the rarest flowers in our garden. I arranged among them some forget-me-nots.

[*Enter* MRS. DARLINGTON, *3 E. R.*]

MRS. DARLINGTON. Why, Helen, you had better go and dress yourself. Mrs. Osgood you are welcome. You are looking very well.

MRS. OSGOOD. I feel well, and with hopes soon to hear from Walter, I try to keep up the best way I can.

HELEN. Mrs. Osgood, you will pardon my leaving you for a short time, but I will soon return.

[*Ex. HELEN, 3 E. L.*]

5

MRS. DARLINGTON. Captain, you have ample time, before our friends come, to go to the post-office and see if we have any letters.

MRS. OSGOOD. O dear Mrs. Darlington, let me take that office, and I may be a lucky messenger and return with a letter from my Walter.

CAPTAIN. Let Mrs. Osgood have her own way, and I will remain with you, darling.

[*Exit* MRS. OSGOOD, *centre door in flat.*]

MRS. DARLINGTON. I pray that we may get some news. Helen, of late, is so melancholy.

CAPTAIN. Fiddle-sticks! pah! always something. Did you, or any one else, ever know of a girl in love but that had melancholy spells?

MRS. DARLINGTON. I had the same spells, but those days have gone by; haven't they, my dear Captain?

CAPTAIN. Everything in this world passes away, but not our love.

MRS. DARLINGTON. (*Pinching* CAPTAIN'S *cheeks.*) Don't be so foolish, you are getting pretty well advanced in years.

CAPTAIN. I don't feel a day older than I did twenty-five years ago.

[*Enter* HELEN, *from 3 E. L. with two bouquets, handing one to her mother and one to her father.*]

HELEN. Where is Mrs. Osgood?

MRS. DARLINGTON. She has gone to the post-office.

HELEN. May she bring some good news.

MRS. DARLINGTON. (*Looking out of back window.*) I see her coming, how frightened she looks.

[*Enter* MRS. OSGOOD *crying, and* JONATHAN *screaming, from C. D. F.*]

JONATHAN. O! O! O! the two grand Turks we just met look like Kriss-Kingles.

CAPTAIN. Why Jonathan, you are dreaming.

JONATHAN. I wish it was a dream, I wish I was home with my Ma, they may come here and murder us all.

MRS. OSGOOD. When I left here to go to the post-office, I met Jonathan, and he called my attention to a carriage that was standing on the road, and two of the strangest looking men at the side of it that I ever saw, both dressed in furs, with long beards, and looking as if they had wigs on. I never was so frightened. And our hero, (*pointing to*

JONATHAN,) commenced screaming, but on our way back they disappeared, and worst of all, I did not get a letter.

JONATHAN. You might well call me a hero, otherwise we both would have been killed. O, Captain! let me sleep with you in your bed to-night. I can see them now, standing in front of our bed. Let them come, I'm no coward. I am going to whittle a big stick.

CAPTAIN. O, this time of year we have a great many foreigners traveling through here to see our scenery. No doubt they were on that errand.

HELEN. I would not care how strange they looked, if only one of them would be my Walter. It is now over two months since we have received any news from him.

MRS. OSGOOD. I guess there is no such good fortune in store for us as to have Walter return so soon as this.

MRS. DARLINGTON. (*Looking out from R. window.*) O! here come our friends.

[*Enter* VILLAGERS, *male and female, from centre door in flat.*]

CAPTAIN. All be welcome.

VILLAGERS. (*All.*) Thank you, sir!

MRS. DARLINGTON. Be merry and make yourselves all at home, ladies and gentlemen. (VILLAGERS *all bow.*)

JONATHAN. By Jove, this is a pretty creature! (*Going towards one of the girls.*) I would not mind to make you Mrs. Jonathan Skinner.

[*Enter* PIERRE LIVINGSTON *and* FREDERICK DARLINGTON.]

PIERRE. Ladies, I am pleased to see you. (*Aside.*) How beautiful she looks.

HELEN. (*Aside.*) I wish that man was not present, I hate him.

MRS. DARLINGTON. Come girls, give us a song.

[VILLAGERS *sing* "*Come let us be Merry on this Happy Day,*" *and* "*Home, Sweet Home.*"]

CAPTAIN. I thank you; now, let us have a dance.

JONATHAN. Captain, when I was at home, and there was a dance in the school-house, the girls would not dance with any other beau but your humble servant, Jonathan Skinner.

CAPTAIN. Well, Jonathan, you shall dance with Mrs. Darlington.

MRS. DARLINGTON. (*Aside.*) Ain't he kind. My old fool to select such a beau for me.

JONATHAN. Mrs. Darlington, I engage you for the dance; and none of your sliding, 'cause I'll kick right up.

[JONATHAN, MRS. DARLINGTON, PIERRE, MRS. OSGOOD, FREDERICK, HELEN, *and others, form a quadrille. Dance over.*]

FREDERICK.   Father, before I came in here I met two strange-looking men, no doubt Russians, they were dressed that way.   I wonder what they were doing in these parts.

CAPTAIN.   Mrs. Osgood has told me of these men, and if they are friendly visitors they are welcome here.

MRS. OSGOOD.   (*Going to R. window.*)   Here they are coming.

JONATHAN.   O, my poor soul, this is my last!   (*Running around the room and shaking and hiding under the table, and every time the strangers speak he looks from under the table, saying*) :—I know they are grand Turks.

[*Enter* WALTER *and* ANDRÉ LIVINGSTON *from C. D. in Flat. disguised with long beards, dressed in Russian costume, with furs on their clothing, and long cloaks.*]

WALTER.   (*To Captain.*)   Pardon, sir, for this intrusion, as we see you have a fête here to-day.

CAPTAIN.   Gentlemen, be welcome, and be our guests to-day. Twenty-five years ago I was married to this lady.   (*Introducing* MRS. DARLINGTON.)

WALTER.   Sir, I, as well as my friend, are under many obligations to you for your cordial invitation, but some important business will prevent us accepting your kind hospitality.

CAPTAIN.   As you seem strangers in these parts, if I can be of any service to you it will afford me much pleasure.   From what part of Europe do you come?

ANDRÉ.   We come from St. Petersburgh.   (HELEN *and* MRS. OSGOOD *draw near.*)

MRS. OSGOOD.   Did you hear those gentlemen say they came from St. Petersburgh.

HELEN.   Let me ask them, they may give us some information in regard to our Walter.

WALTER.   (*Aside.*)   Sweet angel, once more do I hear that sweet voice.

ANDRÉ.   (*To Captain.*)   Sir, as the host here, you have a good many friends assembled to-night.

CAPTAIN.   Yes, on such occasions as this we should always have our friends present.   You will pardon me for a moment.   (*Goes to* PIERRE *and speaks to him.*)   My boy, you will attend to that little matter I spoke to you of this forenoon.

PIERRE.   I will sir, immediately.

ANDRÉ. This young man is a son of yours' no doubt ?

JONATHAN. (*Getting from under the table.*) And I, sir, the adopted baby.

CAPTAIN. Jonathan, be quiet.

JONATHAN. How can I, I feel like I have the delirium tremens.

CAPTAIN. No, sir; he is not my son, but as good as one. He is a friend of my Frederick, his name is Pierre Livingston.

ANDRÉ. (*Aside.*) My God, this is my son!

CAPTAIN. Sir, you seem agitated.

ANDRÉ. No sir, not in the least, some past recollections came to my mind.

CAPTAIN. What is your friend's name ?

ANDRÉ. His name is Emil Howard.

CAPTAIN. And yours?

ANDRÉ. Edward Singleton. The parents of this young man, Pierre Livingston, are no doubt deceased ?

CAPTAIN. His mother died when he was quite young, and his father left him in care of his housekeeper, a Mrs. Blanchard, who since the departure of his father also died. As to the history of his father, he was so young that he has but a faint recollection, but I know his history as well as if it had happened this very day.

WALTER. Mr. Singleton, we must leave ; it is getting late ; and we must attend to that important message.

ANDRÉ. (*Aside to* WALTER) O, God, I cannot stand this any longer ; here is my son, who I have not seen for so many years ; let us take off our disguise.

WALTER. And how must I feel ? I recognize my dear mother ; but not yet ; keep up courage, all will come out right.

[MRS. OSGOOD *approaches* ANDRÉ.]

MRS. OSGOOD. I overheard that you came from St. Petersburgh, and as I have a son there, Walter Osgood, could you give me any information in regard to him ?

HELEN. (*Drawing near.*) O, how kind you are to comply with my wishes.

WALTER. (*Aside.*) How well my dear mother looks. I cannot, nay, I will not longer be in suspense.

ANDRÉ. It would afford me great pleasure if I could inform you in regard to your son, but I have not the honor of knowing him. It may be my friend Mr. Howard can.

WALTER. (*Aside.*) Edward, I cannot longer withhold embracing my mother, after my long absence.

MRS. DARLINGTON. Captain, the conversation with these gentlemen may be all very well, but remember our feast, and let us all be merry.

[WALTER *takes off his disguise aud rushes to his mother.*]

WALTER.   I cannot longer be in suspense; I am your son Walter.

JONATHAN.   By Jove, altered from a grand Turk to son Walter! but that other snapper, he looks Turkey-like, anyhow.

MRS. OSGOOD.   (*Embracing* WALTER.)   Walter, my son, how can I ever forget this day,—to be blessed once more, to behold you in my arms.

HELEN.   (*Running to* WALTER.)   Walter! Thank heaven, my dream has turned out to be a reality, and now we will never be separated again, except in death.

CAPTAIN.   You are a noble man, and worthy of the hand of Helen.

[*The music plays "Home, Sweet Home."*]

ANDRÉ.   My wishes are complete,—to see my friend Walter married to the girl he so devotedly loved.

WALTER.   (*Taking a large wallet from his pocket.*)   Helen, I have kept my promise not to return till I deserved to make you my happy bride.   This book contains the secret I so long wished to obtain, and I have conquered at last.

PIERRE.   (*Advancing to* HELEN *and* WALTER.)   Allow me to congratulate you.   (*Aside.*)   It is all up with me now.

ANDRÉ.   (*Advancing to* PIERRE.)   I see you are pleased with Walter's return.

PIERRE.   O, sir, I am, but—

ANDRÉ.   But what?

PIERRE.   (*Aside to* ANDRE.)   I loved this girl; O, how unfortunate I am.

[CAPTAIN, MRS. DARLINGTON *and* MRS. OSGOOD *advance;* CAPTAIN *takes* HELEN *by the hand and advances to* WALTER.]

CAPTAIN.   Walter, my son, take her, and be blessed.

MRS. OSGOOD.   May Heaven protect you both.

ANDRÉ.   (*Advancing to* WALTER.)   Accept my congratulations, and may your future be blessed, as you well deserve it.

CAPTAIN.   Now let us have a day of joy, and let it be long remembered by us all.

JONATHAN.   Captain, now I am about a nice age to get spliced; but to whom, that's the question.   If I can't do any better, by Jove, I'll marry the old woman, Mrs. Osgood.

ANDRÉ.   It is complete for us all, except our friend, Pierre.

CAPTAIN.   And why not for him ?

ANDRÉ.   Because he has not heard from his father for so many years.

PIERRE.   Then I would be happy.

ANDRÉ.   (*Taking off his disguise without any one noticing.*)   I will no longer bear that name, I am André Livingston, your long absent father.   Come to my arms, Pierre.

[*They embrace.*]

CAPTAIN.   This is as happy a day for me as it was twenty-five years ago.

WALTER.   (*Advancing to front of stage.*)   Now our joy is complete, and let us thank heaven for its blessing, and let us all live in " Hope and Ambition."

[*Orchestra plays Mendelssohn's Wedding March as the curtain drops.*]

THE END.